MONSOON

Uma Krishnaswami

Pictures by **Jamel Akib**

FARRAR STRAUS GIROUX ✳ NEW YORK

To Shaku, who loved the rainy season
—U.K.

For Nancy
—J.A.

GLOSSARY OF HINDI WORDS

Ganesh (GUH-NAYSH)   the elephant-headed Hindu god of beginnings

koel (KOH-YULL)   a songbird with a loud whistling call, noisiest just before the rains

loo   the hot wind that blows through northern India in summer, before the rainy season

neem   a tree of the mahogany family, whose leaves and fruit are used in farming and for medicine

Text copyright © 2003 by Uma Krishnaswami
Illustrations copyright © 2003 by Jamel Akib
All rights reserved
Distributed in Canada by Douglas & McIntyre Ltd.
Printed and bound in the United States of America by Berryville Graphics
Color separations by Prime Digital Media
Typography by Nancy Goldenberg
First edition, 2003
1 3 5 7 9 10 8 6 4 2

Library of Congress Cataloging-in-Publication Data
Krishnaswami, Uma, 1956–
    Monsoon / Uma Krishnaswami ; pictures by Jamel Akib.
        p.   cm.
    Summary: A child describes waiting for the monsoon rains to arrive and the worry that they will not come.
    ISBN 0-374-35015-9
    1. Monsoons—Fiction.   [1. India—Fiction.]   I. Akib, Jamel, ill.   II. Title.
PZ7.K8978 Mo 2003
[E]—dc21

2001054753

All summer we have worn
the scent of dust—
gravelly, grainy, gritty dust—
blowing on the winds and
sprinkling through our clothes and hair.

At breakfast, Papa says,
"When the monsoon rains arrive,
they'll wash this dust away."

Going to the market,
I cross the road with Mummy.
"We need tomatoes," she says,
"and maybe some beans."

We pass the old tea stall.
It clatters with the chink of cups,
hums and thrums with
wondering and worrying.
Will monsoon rains come soon?

The radio crackles with news
of rain showers by the sea.
But that seashore is far from us.

Mummy sighs.
She watches the sky, and she has questions.
"How much will it rain?
How fast, how hard?" She worries
about floods, and so
I worry, too.

And there is another question.
No one dares to ask it.
It hangs in my mind,
as the cry of the crows in the old *neem* tree
hangs in the dust-pink air:
"What if they never come,
those monsoon rains?"

Still, in the afternoon,
as Mummy chops and stirs,
and lunch smells fill the air,
my busy hands fold paper boats.
I crease their crisp white sails.
In my mind I see them float
in oceans of puddles.

Evening falls.
I watch the faces on TV.
Old and young, poor and rich,
all across India,
we wait for rain.
The heat makes me feel
like a crocodile
crouching snap-jawed.

When Papa comes from work,
I run down to meet him.
Across the street people crowd
around the bus-stop shelter.
Between the screeching of brakes
and the scrambling of feet,
I hear excitement.
"Wait! Listen! Was that thunder
or the rumble of an engine?"

At bedtime, Nani tells us tales
of when the monsoon was wetter,
fuller, longer—back in the days before fields
gave way to city streets.
I listen, till her stories
fade to dreams.

Before day breaks, I hear a *koel* sing
long and wild, in a voice
like melting sunshine.
From far away a peacock wails.
I answer him out loud, and startle
everyone awake.

Hot *loo* winds tear through the city.
They rip the paper off billboards
and shred the smiles of movie stars.

I complain, but
Papa smiles and says,
"We need this hot, dry wind
to ripen those sweet mangoes."

Waves of heat dance upon rocks
and shimmer over rooftops.
But by the afternoon, long gray clouds
begin to trail across the sky.

Nani says,
"You'll see. When those partridge-feather
clouds arrive, the monsoon rain will follow."
"Can we go play?" I ask.
She looks up at the sky.
"Don't take too long."

In the hopscotch square we've chalked
in the alley, my brother and I jump
and hop and whirl
to the sound of temple bells,
clanging, clanging.

"Three forward and three back
and no stops in between will make it rain,"
my brother says.
"That's silly," I tell him,
but I try it anyway.

In the street, a taxi driver honks
an angry horn,
but the old cow is tired
and will not move.
Wheels inch around her. We laugh.
The driver frowns
and wags his head at us,
and tears off in a cloud of dust.

As we head home, the sky is filled with full, fat clouds.
The wispy feather trails are gone.
From far away, thunder pounds
a giant heartbeat.
We know. It won't be long.

The wind ruffles the leaves
on the old *neem* tree.

The newspaper man swishes
plastic bags over the day's headlines.

Suddenly it is still,
a stillness filled
with the scent of ripe mangoes,
with promises
of dampness in the air.

Then—oh!—the rain, the perfect rain,
the stretching, sweeping sheet of rain
storms down.

Umbrellas turn into walking forests.
I sigh, and my sigh rides up to the sky.
The raindrops make me laugh out loud,
thudding on earth and rooftops
and on my skin.

Mummy and Nani cross the street
to clink a coin at the feet
of potbellied Ganesh, god of beginnings.

Rivers gush along yesterday's roads.
I dance with the joy of earth's sudden sweet scent.

About the Monsoon

The word *monsoon* comes from an old Arabic word, *mausim*, meaning "season." The monsoon is the season of rain.

For a monsoon to happen, you need blisteringly hot land. Heated air rising off the earth's surface makes room for strong, wet winds to sweep in from the ocean. The winds in South and Southeast Asia blow from the northeast in winter and the southwest in summer. When they pass over the Indian Ocean and the Arabian Sea, they pick up moisture, and get wetter and wetter. Clouds form and are whirled along. Sometimes migrating birds catch a ride, too. The earth's rotation causes the winds to "bend" in giant swirls. Where mountains and landforms block the water-laden winds, rain squeezes down in great sheets.

Northern India and parts of eastern Malaysia get heavy rain from June through September from the southwest monsoon. The southernmost parts of India, Sri Lanka, and most of Southeast Asia get their rain from the northeast monsoon between November and January. Monsoon rains are strongest and most powerful in India and nearby countries and in Southeast Asia. Weaker monsoons, however, do occur in other parts of the world, including Mexico and the southwestern United States.

In India, the monsoon rain helps food crops grow. But the rain also grows art, music, and stories. Old paintings show kings and queens, gods and people watching the sky, waiting for rain. For hundreds of years, composers have written music inspired by the season. One musical *raga*, or "scale," called "Megh Malhaar," is supposed to help bring rain. Classical Indian dances have special hand gestures for rain, others for storms, still others for lightning.

The rains can also be frightening and dangerous. In some places, they come with such force that floods result. Fields and houses are swept away, and sometimes thousands of people are left homeless. Traffic is forced to a halt for days in cities and towns. Businesses have to close. But if the rains don't come at all, the crops will die and there will be no rice, no wheat—no food! And so the monsoon is both loved and feared.